CRABTREE SCHOOL

First published in the UK in 2015 by Scholastic Children's Books
An imprint of Scholastic Ltd
Euston House, 24 Eversholt Street
London, NW1 1DB, UK
Registered office: Westfield Road, Southam, Warwickshire, CV47 0RA
SCHOLASTIC and associated logos are trademarks and/or
registered trademarks of Scholastic Inc.

ISBN 978 1407 15326 1

A CIP catalogue record for this book
is available from the British Library

Printed and bound by CPI Group (UK) Ltd, Croydon, CR0 4YY

Papers used by Scholastic Children's Books are made
from wood grown in sustainable forests.

1 3 5 7 9 10 8 6 4 2

www.scholastic.co.uk

CRABTREE SCHOOL

The Girl Who Stole the World

Lauren Pearson
Illustrated by Becka Moor

SCHOLASTIC

For all the Mums and Dads,
especially mine, who try their best
to teach us right from wrong

And for my little sister, too,
who is nothing like the Reds

Chapter

The Greenest Girl in the World

Isabel Donaldson was going to save planet Earth. There was nothing that could stand in her way. Especially not a five-year-old Reception girl called Lucy Lu Miller.

Lucy Lu had just finished eating a very special ice lolly. It was the kind of ice lolly that is green and pink and white with loads of pink sprinkles on. The kind that tastes like watermelon bubblegum. The kind that you win when your class at Crabtree School for Girls gets lots of golden tickets for being good.

Lucy Lu was walking through the ground

floor hallway of Crabtree School. Her shiny school shoes went *squeak*, *squeak* on the marble floor. Her curly bunches, tied with red ribbons, went *boing boing* as she made her way towards the kitchen. In one chubby little hand, Lucy Lu held the empty wrapper from her lolly. In her other hand, she carried the stick. She had licked it clean.

Isabel knew just where Lucy Lu was going. She followed Lucy into the school lunch room. Mrs Crunch, the dinner lady, was setting out some freshly baked bread on the long tables. Isabel's stomach growled, but she carried on after Lucy Lu, who had stopped in front of the huge bin in the corner.

Lucy Lu was just about to drop the wrapper and the stick from the ice lolly into the bin when Isabel sprang into action.

"STOP!" Isabel cried. Lucy Lu nearly jumped out of her shoes. So did Mrs Crunch, who dropped a whole tray of dishes on the floor with a *crash*!

"YOU MUST STOP NOW TO SAVE THE PLANET!" repeated Isabel. Lucy Lu froze. The lolly wrapper and the stick hovered above the bin. Lucy Lu looked like she might cry at any moment. Being shouted at by a Year Three girl like Isabel was very scary indeed.

"Lucy Lu," said Isabel gently, taking the younger girl by the elbow, "we can recycle that wrapper!" She led Lucy Lu round the corner into a little hallway off the school kitchen, where there were more bins. These bins were brightly coloured.

"Look," said Isabel. "That wrapper is plastic. We can put it in this *blue* bin and then someone can make it into something else. That's what recycling is – did you know that?" Isabel spoke very slowly. She herself was already eight years old, but she had two little sisters. Isabel knew

just how to explain things to much younger children.

"The wrapper is dirty," said Lucy Lu. "Yuck. It goes in the yucky bin." She turned back towards the big bin in the lunch room.

"No!" cried Isabel. "If you just throw everything away in the normal bin, soon the whole world will be filled with rubbish. Then we will have to live on big piles of rubbish, in houses filled with rubbish. We will walk on pavements made of rubbish, drive cars made of rubbish. Everything will be stinky and sticky and—"

Lucy Lu giggled. But Isabel wasn't laughing. She pointed again to the blue bin. She crossed her arms and tapped her foot.

"Lucy Lu," said Isabel. "We have to take care of our planet. Crabtree School is a green school, and we recycle!"

"Crabtree School is RED!" said Lucy Lu,

"not green!" Really, Lucy Lu was correct: Crabtree School was made of red brick.

Isabel sighed. "The COLOUR of Crabtree School is red," she explained to Lucy patiently. "But being a *green* school means that we take care of the planet. We want to keep the planet green."

"What is a planet?" asked Lucy Lu.

This was going to take a long time.

Isabel explained everything to Lucy Lu: the Earth and the moon and the sun and the stars. She explained the universe and the galaxy. Then she told Lucy Lu how the earth was getting poorly and full of rubbish. She described what happens to rubbish when you bin it, and how things are recycled. Isabel talked all about rainforests and endangered animals and dolphins caught by accident in fishermen's nets.

Lucy Lu listened and listened. She asked a million questions. Then she listened some more.

Isabel had begun to lose her voice from talking so much when Lucy Lu heard shouts from the playground. The rest of her class was outside and she was missing playtime.

At last, Lucy Lu shrugged and dropped the plastic wrapper and the stick into the blue recycling bin.

"WAIT!" screeched Isabel. "The stick is wood! It doesn't go in with the plastic!" Isabel had planned to teach Lucy Lu all about the different bins, but Lucy Lu had already turned to walk away.

Isabel reached into the blue bin to retrieve the stick. The bin was mostly empty, so Isabel had to lean down to get the stick at the bottom. Suddenly, the bin tipped forward, and then back again. Isabel lost her balance. Her feet came off the ground and before she knew it, she was upside down at the bottom of the recycling bin.

At that very moment she heard a muffled voice above her.

"Why, Miss Lucy Lu," said this voice. It was Mrs Peabody, the headmistress of Crabtree School. "Look at you recycling! What a good girl! Now let's get you back outside with your class." Isabel heard their footsteps fading away together.

Mrs Peabody hadn't seen Isabel fall into the bin, but someone else had. After a moment, two

huge brown eyes peered down at Isabel. It was Lottie, Isabel's best friend. Isabel wasn't at all surprised to see her. Lottie always seemed to be everywhere at once, poking her nose into everyone else's business. Or into their bin.

"Are you recycling YOURSELF?" asked Lottie, as she tipped the bin over so Isabel could climb out. Lottie was definitely going to record this incident in her purple notebook; she had already taken it out of her pocket. Lottie wrote everything down in it, like a proper spy. Isabel liked the idea that Lottie made lots of lists, for Isabel loved a list. But Lottie's handwriting could have been better, she noticed. Isabel herself had perfect penmanship.

"Good thing the bin was empty!" Isabel stood, holding up the wooden stick from Lucy Lu's lolly. "This was easy to find and it's perfect for my collection!"

"You sure are good at recycling," said Lottie,

as Isabel tucked the lolly stick into her dress pocket. "You must be the greenest girl in all the world!"

"Yes, probably," said Isabel proudly. "Now we'd better get to class, or we'll be late." Isabel had never been late for school or to class, not a single time in more than three years at Crabtree School, and she wasn't about to start now.

Chapter

2

Which Colour Bin Should
Little Sisters Go in?

Isabel had a little-sister problem. She had two of them, actually. Their names were Ruby and Scarlett. They were three-and-a-half years old, and they were twins. Isabel's daddy called them the Reds. He called them that because of their names, which both meant red, and not because they had red hair. The Reds had yellow hair, and huge blue eyes and sweet little pink mouths. They looked like two tiny angels.

Except the Reds were not angels. The Reds were the naughtiest little sisters in the whole history of little sisters. Anything that you can

11

think of that naughty little sisters did, the Reds did it naughtier. They pulled hair. They threw food. They hid the TV remote so Isabel couldn't watch anything but *Peppa Pig*. They filled her wellies with mud pies. They dipped her toothbrush into the toilet and put their socks in her spaghetti.

The Reds especially loved everything that was Isabel's. They dressed up in her clothes and made them all messy. They played with her toys and lost all the pieces. They left the tops off all of her markers so they dried out.

In fact, the Reds were downright dangerous with markers. They'd once coloured Isabel's pet rabbit bright pink. It had taken four baths to make Cottontail white again. Even worse, the pink marker had got all clogged up with rabbit fur. It had had to go in the bin.

Even Isabel's friends were scared of the Reds. Not long ago, the Reds had scribbled all over

Lottie's secret notebook and ruined years of her spy work.

Everyone knew it was best to steer clear of Isabel's little sisters.

So when Isabel got home that afternoon with Lucy Lu's ice lolly stick, she went straight to her room. It would be more difficult for the Reds to bother her there.

Even though she was eight years old, Isabel was not allowed to have a lock on her bedroom door. Locks can get stuck and trap you inside. They can make people feel left out. They can even be dangerous if there is a fire. For all these reasons, Isabel had to agree with her mummy that a lock on her bedroom door was not a good idea.

Besides, Isabel didn't need locks. She had come up with her own way of keeping the Reds out. When she left her room each morning, Isabel put a piece of tape on the outside of her door. The Reds couldn't reach it. Even if they could, they weren't allowed to take it off. Isabel's mummy had told them that if the tape was broken or peeled off or moved or breathed on, then the Reds would have no sweeties FOREVER. This was scary enough that, although they spent a lot of time staring at the tape on Isabel's door, the Reds had never dared to touch it. As long as she remembered the tape, the Reds did not go in Isabel's room when she wasn't there.

Isabel pulled off that morning's tape and closed the door behind her. Then she hung a jingle bell from last Christmas over the doorknob. This was so she could hear if the Reds tried to break in. Next, Isabel pushed her fuzzy pink rug right up against the bottom of her door, which made it difficult to open. Then she took one of the chairs from her craft table and put that on top of the pink rug; the

Reds were still small and the chair was too heavy for them to push out of the way. Finally, Isabel put her heaviest teddy on the chair. He added extra weight and also kept watch.

The Reds could hardly be blamed for wanting to get into Isabel's room. There were so many amazing things in there that even the best-behaved little sisters would have been pounding down the door trying to get inside.

Isabel loved crafts. She loved building things, drawing things, sewing things, colouring things, sticking things, folding things and melting things. Her room was full of the wonderful art that she had created. There were little people made out of conkers living in her doll's house. There were crazy eggshell heads with bean sprouts for hair lined up on her bedside table. Her windows were covered with leaves that Isabel had painted red and orange and sprinkled with red glitter. The glitter sparkled in the sunlight.

Isabel also loved tidiness. Everything had its place: the shelves and bins around Isabel's craft table held jars with markers (new ones, to replace all the ones the Reds had ruined), crayons, fancy oil pens and moulding clay. There were empty boxes of all shapes and sizes, toilet-paper rolls, strips of newspaper for papier mâché, all different colours of elastic bands, stones and rocks and conkers, sticks, pipe cleaners, paper clips, empty bottles, bits of thread and ribbon and wire, folded crisp wrappers, dried flowers and leaves...

It would actually take a whole day to write down all the things that Isabel saved. (Lottie had tried it once. She wanted to make a list in the ISABEL section of her purple notebook. She had given up after two hours when her hand got tired.)

Isabel took Lucy Lu's ice lolly stick and

added it to the jar that held loads of other ice lolly sticks. When winter came, Isabel was going to glue the sticks together and cover them with glitter to make snowflakes. She'd done a few snowflakes last year and they had come out really twinkly and lovely.

With the lolly stick tidied away, Isabel opened her school bag and took out her spelling homework. She always did her homework as soon as she got home from school, because that was the right thing to do. And it worked, too. Isabel had never got a single word wrong on a spelling test, ever.

When she'd finished practising the final bonus word from her spelling list (it was *hideous*, which means very ugly), Isabel set to work on her latest craft project.

By far, this was going to be the greatest thing Isabel had ever made. In one corner of her room, Isabel was building a giant, playhouse-sized igloo out of plastic milk containers. Right now, she was about halfway through gluing the containers together in a big circle. It took ages, because you had to hold each container in place for a long time whilst the glue set, but Isabel didn't mind. She loved watching

the walls get higher and higher. They were at knee height already. She worked away at her gluing until the bell on her bedroom door began to jingle.

"Izzy!" shrieked Scarlett. "Let us in. Can we play with you?"

"Please, Izzy, please!!!" cried Ruby.

The bell jingled and jingled and the door began to shake on its hinges. The teddy fell from his chair.

Isabel sighed. She got up and moved the chair and the rug. The Reds bounded into the room and stood before Isabel's igloo.

"Wow!!!" They gasped. For a minute, the Reds stood still, admiring it. Then they went back to causing trouble.

"Let's make it pink!" suggested Ruby, looking round for Isabel's markers.

"No!" cried Isabel. She scrambled around trying to grab the markers from them.

"We want to help you!" pleaded Scarlett. She picked up the tub of glue, spilling some on the carpet. She began to spread loads of glue on a milk container.

"That's too much glue!" shrieked Isabel. "I told you, puddles are for ducks, not glue!" But Scarlett had already made an ocean of glue, and it was running down her arms and on to the igloo. This was too much for Isabel to take.

"I don't need any help!" screeched Isabel. "And you are doing it all wrong! The containers have to line up properly or the igloo won't be right!" The side of the igloo was dangerously close to collapsing. She'd have to start over! Isabel wondered how much trouble she would get into if she glued the Reds together.

Luckily her dad came to the rescue before Isabel had to break any rules.

"Izzy, that is quite an igloo!" he said, popping his head in the door. "A whole family of

Eskimos could move in there!"

Isabel's daddy had just come home from work. When he saw that the igloo was under attack from the Reds, he put one twin over each shoulder and carried them out of Isabel's room. Ruby still had a marker in her hand. Isabel watched as she made a long pink scribble across the back of their dad's white shirt. His hair was covered in glue from Scarlett's sticky hands.

When they were safely gone, Isabel looked at the drippy igloo, which was now leaning to one side. For the millionth time that week, she wondered how any two three-year-olds could be that naughty. Isabel certainly never had been. Her mum was always saying to other grown-ups that Isabel was born well-behaved. Then she would laugh about how then she got her naughty twins, to make up for having such an angelic daughter. Isabel couldn't understand why her mummy smiled when she said this. There was nothing funny about being naughty.

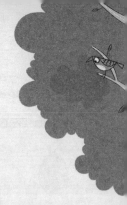

Chapter

Mirror, Mirror on the Wall, Who Is the Greenest of Them All?

The next day, there was a surprise assembly at Crabtree School for Girls. Even Lottie hadn't known anything about it until earlier that morning, when she happened to be sitting under the headmistress's desk and overheard Mrs Peabody talking.

The entire school gathered in the playground: the girls, the teachers, Mrs Biro the school secretary, the dinner lady Mrs Crunch and her husband, Colonel Crunch, who looked after the school grounds. Lady Lovelypaws, the school cat, was there too, perched on top of the slide.

A stage had been set up beneath two crab apple trees. The girls were sitting in neat rows on the grass. It was a glorious crisp autumn day, and everyone was happy to be out in the fresh air. Isabel was sitting between Lottie, who was so full of secret information that she was ready to burst, and their friend Ava.

"Maybe an alien school is coming to visit us?" suggested Ava. Ava had a wild imagination. "Maybe we are all waiting out here to greet the school bus spaceship!"

"Shh!" Isabel told her. "You really shouldn't talk in assembly."

Before Ava could reply, Mrs Peabody stepped up on the stage. Mrs Peabody was known throughout Great Britain to be the kindest headmistress at any school anywhere. She loved Crabtree School. She adored each and every girl who went there. She loved every teacher and every brick, each and every crab apple tree and every last blade of grass. Today Mrs Peabody wore a bright green dress and her hair was especially fluffy and soft. Isabel thought it looked like cotton wool. The headmistress's cheeks were rosy with excitement, as if they had been coloured with a red marker.

"Girls!" cried Mrs Peabody. "I have such delightful news! Such wonderful, stupendous news!"

Everyone went quiet.

"We've ... it's... Oh my!" Mrs Peabody went on, "Mrs Potion has just told me ... she's told me..."

"I told you," Ava whispered to Isabel. "The aliens are coming! Mrs Potion has a telescope so she has probably seen them!"

Mrs Potion taught Year Five, so Isabel made sure to smile and say hello to Mrs Potion when she passed her in the hallway. Mrs Potion would be their teacher in two years' time, and it was never too early to get on your teacher's good side.

Whatever Mrs Potion had said to Mrs Peabody was so exciting that the headmistress couldn't bring herself to repeat it. Next to her, Mrs Potion was jumping up and down.

"Crabtree School has ... we've..."

Lottie could stand it no more.

"CRABTREE SCHOOL HAS WON THE *Our Beautiful Green Planet Intergalactic Environmental Award*!" Lottie shouted.

There were shouts and cheers all around, *hoorays* and *well done*s from every corner of the playground.

Then, from a few places down from Isabel, a timid hand was raised.

"Yes, Rani?" said Mrs Peabody. Rani was the new girl at Crabtree School. She was in Year Three and Isabel liked her very much. Last week, Rani had even come round to Isabel's house with Ava, Zoe and Lottie to help Isabel begin work on the igloo.

"Sorry, Mrs Peabody," said Rani. "But what is the *Our Beautiful Green Planet Intergalactic Environmental Award?*"

"It's ... well ... it's ... I don't know exactly," said Mrs Peabody. "But isn't it wonderful?"

Everyone nodded as Mrs Potion hurried to explain.

"We've won the *Our Beautiful Green Planet Intergalactic Environmental Award* because we take such wonderful care of our beautiful green planet here at Crabtree School. How do we do that, girls?"

Isabel put her hand up. "We recycle!" she said proudly.

"That's right!" said Mrs Potion. "What else?"

Isabel put her hand up again, but Mrs Potion decided to give someone else a turn. At Crabtree School, the Green Thumb Club grew fruit and vegetables for school dinners. The Crabtree School Jolly Neighbourhood Helpers Club helped tidy Crabtree Park across the street. Lots of Crabtree girls walked to school, or took the bus or came by bicycle or scooter, instead of coming in the car. All of these things were good for the planet.

"Those are all correct, girls!!" said Mrs Potion. "And because we work so hard at being green, Crabtree School has been given this special award by the mayor!"

Mrs Potion held up a golden ball. It was about the size of an apple, and it shone in the sunlight. It was the *Our Beautiful Green Planet Intergalactic Environmental Award* trophy.

"I'll pass it round, girls," said Mrs Potion, "but be very careful! It is made of real gold." She put it gently into the hands of a Reception girl sitting in the front row.

"AND NOW," Mrs Potion continued, "we

also want to acknowledge one special Crabtree student. According to Mrs Peabody, this girl goes well and truly beyond what any of us would expect in her love for our planet."

Isabel straightened up in her seat. There was no one at Crabtree School that loved the planet more than Isabel.

"This girl," said Mrs Peabody, "is a shining example to all of us here. And in two weeks' time, she will get to meet the mayor. The mayor is coming to Crabtree School to officially present the award!"

Isabel had butterflies fluttering in her stomach. She was nervous and excited all at the same time. The golden ball was making its way down the row towards her. She could see now that it was a globe; yes, the ball was a beautiful golden planet Earth and she, Isabel, had helped to win it. Mrs Peabody was going to say her name at any moment: Isabel

Donaldson. Isabel held her breath.

"And even though this girl is one of the smallest among us," Mrs Peabody continued, "she is very grown-up when it comes to recycling!"

Now wait just one minute. That didn't sound right. Isabel was the second tallest girl in Year Three. She was taller than all of Year Two and all of Year One and all of Reception. Why would Mrs Peabody call her small?

"I'm so proud of this little lady," Mrs Peabody gushed. "To have only just started at Crabtree School this autumn and still find her way to the recycling bins all on her own!"

Isabel felt a bit sick.

"Our Crabtree School Green Planet Golden Girl," said Mrs Peabody proudly, "and the girl who will get to give the mayor a tour of our school in two weeks' time is…"

Ava thrust the golden ball into Isabel's hands

just as Mrs Peabody said, "Lucy Lu Miller!"

Isabel Donaldson had not won. Lucy Lu Miller, who didn't even know what a planet was, had won instead.

Isabel was so shocked that she dropped the world.

The golden globe rolled under the chair in front of her. Hot tears sprang to Isabel's eyes as the girls in the seats around her gasped and scrambled under their chairs to save the planet.

Isabel herself didn't move. For even though it was shiny and real gold and a proper special award from the mayor, the *Our Beautiful Green Planet Intergalactic Environmental Award* trophy suddenly didn't look so beautiful after all.

Chapter

A Green-Eyed Monster Is Born

Isabel took one last slurp of her juice carton. They'd just come home from school, and her mum was looking through the refrigerator. Isabel could see her reward chart taped to the refrigerator door, shining with dozens of gold stars. Isabel had earned nearly one hundred stars for doing her chores, having good manners, being kind to her sisters, practising piano, and looking after the pet bunnies. She had done a lot more good things than the Reds had. Their chart hung below Isabel's, and between them, Scarlett and Ruby had a total of three stars.

As she stood there, Isabel noticed that her mum had forgotten to give her a star for practising the piano yesterday. There was also a blank space for clearing the table this morning, which Isabel had done without being asked. Her mum was ALWAYS forgetting stars, unless they were for the Reds. When the Reds got a star, her mum practically had a party for them. It wasn't fair at all.

"I'm sorry, Izzy," said her mum when Isabel pointed out the missing stickers. "But you are so good all the time, such a lovely big girl, that I don't think you need rewarding so much now. Maybe we don't need your star chart any more?"

No stars? It was as if her mummy had suggested they didn't need air to breathe, or food to eat.

"Why do I get my stars taken away for being GOOD?" cried Isabel. "That's not fair!"

"I didn't mean that, Izzy," said her mum. "If it is that important to you we will carry on with them." Her mum got out two stickers and added them to Isabel's chart, but Isabel was still cross. What was the point of being good if no one noticed? Not her mum, not Mrs Peabody...

Isabel looked down at the empty juice carton in her hand. It was made of cardboard, and it belonged in the recycling bin. But why should Isabel bother?

After a quick glance around, Isabel dropped the juice carton into the normal bin. Mrs Peabody wasn't there to see this terrible act, and Isabel's mum didn't pay any attention. The Reds were emptying the contents of a cupboard on to the floor. No one cared that Isabel hadn't recycled.

Isabel reached into the recycling bin and took out an aluminium soup tin. She tossed it loudly into the regular bin.

No one noticed.

Isabel walked over to the kitchen tap. She turned it on. She walked back to the bins and looked for more things to un-recycle. She thought about all of the water that she was wasting.

After ages and ages, Isabel's mummy took her head out of the fridge. "We've absolutely no food left in the house!" she said. "Izzy, darling, you've left the tap on."

"Who cares?" said Isabel crossly.

"Who cares?" is a very rude thing to say to your mummy. At any other time, Isabel's mum would have been shocked to hear her most well-behaved child say such a naughty thing. But emptying an entire box of cereal on to the floor is also very naughty, and that is precisely what Scarlett did at that very moment.

Scarlett and Mummy began to clean up the cereal together, and Isabel's rudeness was forgiven and forgotten. The juice carton and the soup tin stayed in the normal bin. The water from the tap ran on and on. And no one cared, especially not Isabel. She did not care one tiny little bit.

Back in her room, with her door secured against the Reds, Isabel did not do her spelling homework. Instead she set straight to work on the igloo. Her mum had washed loads more milk cartons out and they needed gluing. She hadn't got very far when the Red alarm began to jingle.

"Go away!" shouted Isabel. "I mean it!"

But they didn't. The Reds jingled and pushed and pleaded with Isabel. The Red alarm wasn't working very well these days. Finally, with a great sigh, Isabel moved the teddy and the chair and the rug and the bell. In came the Reds and they headed straight for the igloo.

They jumped around it and climbed over it. They broke off two containers – two containers that had taken ages to glue. Then the Reds went for the markers. They still wanted to colour the igloo.

Isabel shouted for her mum, but her mum didn't come.

Angry butterflies fluttered in Isabel's tummy again. It wasn't fair for the Reds to wreck her igloo. Why did littlies get away with EVERYTHING? She watched them poking at the igloo. She wanted to grab their arms and drag them out of her room. She wanted to push them out and slam the door and lock it forever and ever with a real lock. But then she'd get into trouble. Maybe she'd even lose stars from her chart. And the Reds wouldn't, because they hardly had any stars to lose. It just wasn't fair.

Then she got an idea.

"I know what we can do with the markers," Isabel said to her sisters. She led them over to her craft table and took down her best new markers. They were the permanent kind, and they were scented.

"We do the igloo?" asked Ruby.

"No," Isabel told her. "I have a much better plan." For Isabel had decided that perhaps the way to get noticed for doing good things was to do some really awful things too, every once in a while. It was risky, but it seemed to work for the Reds.

The three sisters coloured away happily for nearly an hour. They were so quiet that Isabel's mum came to check on them.

"ISABEL ELIZABETH DONALDSON! WHAT ON EARTH ARE YOU DOING?" Isabel's mum shouted.

Even though she had the two naughtiest toddlers in the world, Isabel's mummy did not shout very often. She had once been a teacher, and she was patient and kind. She only really shouted when she was very surprised.

Which was now. Isabel's mummy was VERY surprised to find her three blonde daughters with hair streaked every colour of the rainbow.

Scarlett had coloured Ruby's hair in shades of orange and green, and Ruby had chosen purple and blue for Scarlett. Isabel had done her own hair mostly pink; the twins had helped her with the places she couldn't quite reach. Then they'd all sprinkled glitter over their heads because it turns out sparkles look as good in your hair as they do on your windows.

Isabel's mummy stared. "Girls, what have you done?" she demanded. "And why do I smell strawberries?" The whole room smelt of scented markers.

They all stood looking at each other. Isabel's mummy was getting ready to be very angry.

So angry that it was taking her a while to get started.

Then Isabel's daddy came in. He said that the three of them looked like they were in a band. He laughed and laughed. He said he couldn't help himself, because they looked so funny. Finally Isabel's mummy laughed too. The Reds sang and Isabel pretended to play the drums.

After quite a few songs from the band, which they decided was called "Izzy and the Red Rainbow-Heads", they went downstairs for dinner.

At bath time they discovered that Cottontail had been a lucky bunny. It took *way* more than four washes to get marker pen out of people's hair. For many weeks afterwards, Isabel's plaits had a pink glow and smelt of bubblegum.

But they'd got away with it. Isabel and the Reds had been naughty and they didn't get into trouble. Not at all. In fact, it had been fun. And Isabel hadn't even lost any stars.

As Isabel lay in bed that night, breathing in the scent of bubblegum marker, she thought about how she hadn't been in real trouble for a long time. She was the best-behaved girl in her class. She was the best-behaved girl at Crabtree School.

But really, thought Isabel, *who cares?*

Did anyone care? Was there any point to being good when no one noticed and being naughty was so much more fun?

When she finally fell asleep, Isabel dreamt of running taps and of trying to colour Lucy Lu Miller's bouncing bunches with a green marker pen.

Chapter

Butterflies Love Red Ice Lollies

The next morning Isabel wore purple socks with her school uniform. The girls were supposed to wear white socks with their Crabtree uniforms, but Isabel chose fuzzy purple knee-high socks instead, just to see what would happen. Purple socks were much more fun, and Isabel knew that her friends would like them.

"Izzy, are you allowed to wear those socks to school?" asked her mummy at breakfast.

"Yes," Isabel lied. "It is Special Sock Day today."

Her mummy believed her. She had no reason

not to, for Isabel was her good girl. Isabel's mum had already forgotten about last night's naughtiness.

When Isabel walked up the path to Crabtree School that morning, the butterflies were fluttering in her tummy again; in fact, they felt a bit like wasps buzzing. Surely Mrs Peabody would notice her socks and make her change? Isabel's hair was still pink too. Maybe she looked so wild and crazy that Mrs Peabody would send her home? Isabel opened the door with shaky hands and stepped into the school's front hall.

Mrs Peabody was there to greet everyone, just as she was every morning. She was standing next to the statue of Lady Constance Hawthorne, the very first headmistress of Crabtree School for Girls. At Lady Hawthorne's feet was her little stone dog, Baron Biscuit. Isabel could see that Mrs Peabody was admiring something on a pedestal next to the Baron.

It was the *Our Beautiful Green Planet Intergalactic Environmental Award* trophy. On the same pedestal as the award was a picture of Crabtree School's Green Planet Golden Girl, Lucy Lu Miller.

Isabel and her purple socks went up the stairs to the Year Three classroom.

"Are we allowed to wear purple socks now?" Lottie asked Isabel. "I didn't know that."

"No," said Isabel. "I just felt like it." Lottie stared as Isabel sat down at her desk in the front row of the classroom. She watched as Isabel stretched her legs and her purple socks out in front of her, right under their teacher's nose.

"Isabel, you look colourful today!" said Miss Moody.

Miss Moody liked to see Isabel bend the rules sometimes. She thought that being good and proper absolutely all the time must be hard for

Isabel. So Miss Moody did not bother about Isabel's socks.

"Do I smell bubblegum in here, girls?" said Miss Moody, sniffing the air. "Please remember that there is no bubblegum allowed in school, except for on special occasions. Now, let's start with our science lesson!"

Isabel did not get in trouble for her purple socks or her bubblegum pink plaits.

In fact, it turned out that Isabel was very good at doing naughty things and not getting punished. And it turned out that naughty things were quite fun.

At lunchtime, it was Year Two's turn to have ice lollies for their golden ticket reward. Isabel watched them queuing up for their treat. She thought of all the good things she herself had done to win golden tickets for Year Three. She had written her homework extra neatly, kept her PE kit tidy, been quiet whilst queuing up, helped Colonel Crunch water the flowers on the playground... But Year Three still had not collected enough golden tickets to have ice lollies. That was because not everyone in Year Three was as good and helpful as Isabel.

Which wasn't fair really, when you thought about it.

With the butterflies fluttering in her tummy again – butterflies must like ice lollies – Isabel joined the Year Two queue. Mrs Crunch was handing out bright red lollies with white sprinkles. The kind that tasted like strawberries and cream. The kind that were Isabel's absolute favourite type of ice lolly. Keeping her head down so Mrs Crunch wouldn't notice that she didn't belong there, Isabel took one.

Miss Cheeky, the Year Two teacher, didn't notice Isabel eating her illegal ice lolly in the corner until one of the Year Two girls told on her. Miss Cheeky was busy shooing her class

into the toilets to wash their sticky hands. She made a frowny face and wagged her finger at Isabel, which made the tummy butterflies go mad.

Then Miss Cheeky winked. She wasn't *really* cross. Like Miss Moody, Miss Cheeky was pleased to see Isabel, who was always so good and mild-mannered, do something a little bit, well, *cheeky*.

Isabel threw the lolly stick and the wrapper in the normal bin in the lunch room, which was another naughty thing. But by now, Isabel had figured out that being naughty had its own rewards, and not just an ice lolly. After lunch, Isabel marched right to the front of the Year Three queue to go outside. She pushed in front of Zoe, who was so surprised to see Isabel be rude and break the rules that she didn't even tell on her. Isabel got to be first out on to the playground.

Then, during break, Isabel did something she had secretly wanted to do for ages: she made daisy chains. You weren't supposed to pick the flowers that grew around the playground. They were for everyone at Crabtree School to look at and enjoy. But no one was watching, and so Isabel convinced Ava that they should make bracelets and crowns and belts. The two friends were dripping with daisies, and by the time break was over, there wasn't a single daisy left growing in Colonel Crunch's beloved flower bed.

When the bell rang to go inside, Ava felt guilty. She hid her daisies in the tree house, in a sad, wilted pile. But Isabel was brave, and kept her daisy jewellery on. She knew she wouldn't get in any trouble. All Miss Moody said as she led her class back into the school was, "Isabel, don't you look just like a flower fairy!"

Isabel had broken the school dress code. She had sneaked an ice lolly and jumped a queue. She had made the Crabtree School playground a lot less beautiful.

But all this was nothing compared to what she did next.

Chapter

The Trouble with Sticky Fingers

On her way back to Year Three, Isabel did not bother to keep up with her class. She wandered slowly through the school's front hall. She stood before the *Our Beautiful Green Planet Intergalactic Environmental Award* trophy and studied the photograph of Lucy Lu Miller. The caption under the photo read *Our Green Planet Golden Girl: Lucy Lu Miller, Reception.* Lucy Lu had a huge smile on her face in the picture. She was proudly holding the golden globe, like she had won it all on her own.

But she hadn't. Isabel had won it, really. There

MRS PEABODY

had been a little help from the rest of the school, of course, but mostly it was Isabel.

Who went round the tables after lunch and gathered up plastic for the blue bin? Who took home every single lolly stick and milk carton she could get her hands on, and made them into beautiful art? Who made sure that everyone turned the taps off when they finished washing their hands, sometimes even before they'd rinsed the soap off?

Isabel Donaldson, that's who.

That should have been Isabel's photo there. That real gold award was really Isabel's. And she hadn't even got a proper look at it yet.

Isabel glanced around the hallway. Mrs Peabody's office door was open a crack. Isabel could hear her offering a triple-chocolate biscuit to someone inside; Mrs Peabody loved to invite girls in for a chat and some biscuits. She really was the kindest of the kind.

Next door in the school office, Mrs Biro was bent over her computer, clicking away on the keyboard. She was busy writing important letters to the Crabtree mummies and daddies.

On Isabel's left, Lady Constance Hawthorne stared straight ahead, her stony eyes looking out towards the front door.

No one else was in the hallway. Isabel was alone. She reached out to touch the *Our Beautiful Green Planet Intergalactic Environmental Award* trophy. Real gold felt smooth and cold. She thought she might like to hold the globe, just for a minute. It was heavier than she remembered.

Isabel was about to put the globe back down again when she noticed that her fingers, which were still sticky from the ice lolly and also covered in daisy juice, had left smudges on the real gold.

She began to rub the globe with her sleeve,

to get the sticky off. But rubbing didn't help: the sticky smudges just got covered with fuzz from her cardigan. Isabel rubbed harder. She couldn't put the golden globe back all hairy and yucky. Should she take it to the toilets and wash it off?

Before she could do that, lots of things happened all at once.

Colonel Crunch came marching through the front door with a basket of apples. He was taking them to Mrs Crunch in the kitchen so that she could make her famous apple crumble for tomorrow's pudding.

At the exact same time, loads of ghosts and goblins began pouring out of the assembly room right towards Isabel. The Reception girls had been practising for their Halloween play and they still had their costumes on.

Isabel froze. She closed her fingers around the golden globe in the palm of her hand. She looked in fear at the spot on the pedestal where the globe was meant to be. She had to put it back before anyone saw.

But someone had already seen. Lady Lovelypaws had been watching the golden globe ever since Mrs Peabody put it on display. The cat was hoping that maybe this thing all the humans were fussing over was a mouse. Lady Lovelypaws had never actually caught a mouse before. She hadn't even seen one up close. But if this did turn out to be a real, true-life mouse, Lady Lovelypaws was ready for it. All morning she had kept a half-closed but careful eye on the globe from the top of the stairs.

When the globe began to move (because Isabel moved it), Lady Lovelypaws was *certain* it was a mouse. She didn't know that mice aren't made of real gold and cardigan fuzz. Lady Lovelypaws took a minute to finish her morning bath and then sprang to catch it.

Which meant that suddenly, a big white fluffy thing landed right on the pedestal in front of Isabel! This hairy, squirming animal sent Lucy Lu's photograph crashing to the floor. The frame broke into a million pieces.

"Ahhhh," screamed Isabel in terror. Colonel Crunch dropped his basket of apples all over the floor as Lady Lovelypaws scrambled off the pedestal, knocking it over. The panicked cat jumped over Baron Biscuit's head and disappeared into Mrs Peabody's office to hide in her paper tray. Miss Tiny, the Reception teacher, rushed to steer her class around the rolling apples and broken glass in the hall.

Isabel couldn't very well put the *Our Beautiful Green Planet Intergalactic Environmental Award* golden trophy back now, could she? A colonel or a teacher or a ghost or a goblin might see her.

Isabel could have just dropped the award

amongst the mess on the floor. No one would have noticed. In the commotion that followed the cat crash, Colonel Crunch and Mrs Peabody and Mrs Biro were all looking for the globe. They thought that Lady Lovelypaws had knocked it off the pedestal when she jumped. Isabel could have pretended to find it. She could have just handed it over.

But that's not what she did. What Isabel DID do was to stuff the *Our Beautiful Green Planet*

Intergalactic Environmental Award trophy into her cardigan pocket. Her heart beat fast, and the butterflies did cartwheels in her stomach. The *Our Beautiful Green Planet Intergalactic Environmental Award* was hers.

She hurried away to wash her sticky hands.

Chapter

A Pocket Full of Trouble

Isabel stood in front of the mirror in the school toilets. In the reflection she could see the round top of the *Our Beautiful Green Planet Intergalactic Environmental Award* golden trophy poking out of her pocket.

What had just happened? What had Isabel done?

She'd taken something, that's what. Something that didn't belong to her. Was that stealing? Had Isabel just *stolen* something? She felt a buzz in her stomach, as if the butterflies had invited some wasps over for a party.

Yes, she decided. It was stealing. Isabel had done the naughtiest thing she could possibly think of. She was a thief, a stealer, a taker, a villain. In a film, she would be the baddie that everyone was afraid of.

She looked at her reflection more closely, to see if she looked different than she had earlier in the day. Would everyone be able to tell what she had done?

Isabel had the same blue eyes, the same small nose with its neat rows of freckles. Her pink plaits looked the same. (They smelled the same, too. The sweet bubblegum scent was beginning to make Isabel feel sick.)

No, she thought. *No one will be able to tell*. The location of the *Our Beautiful Green Planet Intergalactic Environmental Award* would be her secret. She would keep it all to herself, just for a little while. Because way deep down, Isabel knew that she could get away with anything.

Isabel took some toilet tissue and stuffed it in her pocket, tucking it around the globe so that no one could see the shiny gold. There. That looked fine. Her gran always had loads of tissues in her pocket, so why shouldn't Isabel?

She buttoned her cardigan. Then she thought about it some more and unbuttoned it. In her tummy, the wasps were going mad. Isabel was afraid that people might actually *see* them buzzing inside her if her cardigan was pulled too tightly across her belly.

She waited there for a minute more, thinking.

She would put it back later. That's what she'd do. Probably no one would even miss it. No one would even care it was gone. But she would know that she'd got to have it all to herself for a little while.

As Isabel passed back through the hallway on her way up to Year Three, Mrs Peabody and Colonel Crunch were on their knees looking for the lost award.

The wasps went bonkers, but Isabel kept going.

That afternoon was the Year Three spelling test. Normally Isabel loved spelling tests, because she always knew all the words, even the bonus words. You could learn just about anything if you practised it every day.

Except Isabel hadn't practised yesterday. Would she get one wrong? For the first time ever?

The *Our Beautiful Green Planet Intergalactic Environmental Award* trophy was still in Isabel's pocket, covered with toilet tissue. She'd thought about stuffing it into her desk, but moving it seemed risky. If she put it in her school bag, she might forget it and her mum would find it. Besides, she needed to keep it handy so that she could put it back, eventually. Seeing the headmistress crawling around on the floor had made Isabel realize that someone *did* care about the Our Beautiful Green Planet Intergalactic Environmental Award. Isabel couldn't keep the globe forever.

Isabel made a plan to put it back: she was going to go to the downstairs toilet after the test. That way she could pass through the hallway and if no one was looking—

"OK, girls," said Miss Moody. "Take out your papers and pencils and get ready for the first word!"

The first word was *take*. That was easy. Isabel wrote it down in her neatest handwriting:

take.

They did a few more words and Isabel began to relax. Then came the bonus words. You got an extra point for these words, and a golden ticket for the jar if you got them all right.

"*Curious*," said Miss Moody. *Was that with*

i-o-u-s or u-o-u-s? Isabel wrote:

cuviuos.

It looked correct.

Next to her, Rani sneezed.

"Bless you, Rani!" said Miss Moody. "Do you need a tissue?"

Rani did need a tissue. But the box of tissues on Miss Moody's desk was empty.

"Oh dear," said Miss Moody. "Too many runny noses this week! Does anyone have a tissue for Rani?"

"Miss Moody, Isabel has tissues," said Lottie helpfully. "I can see loads of them right there in her pocket!" Lottie was sitting behind Isabel. She had clearly been watching Isabel's pocket. Just how much had Lottie seen?

Did Lottie know what Isabel had done?

Isabel panicked. The wasps in her tummy buzzed and stung. Isabel was the kindest, most helpful girl at Crabtree School, but there was

no way that Rani was getting one shred of the tissue from Isabel's pocket. Isabel needed all of it to cover up her guilty secret.

"MIND YOUR OWN BUSINESS!" she shrieked at Lottie.

It was not like Isabel to shout at her friend. Lottie was shocked. But Isabel had other things to worry about.

"Rani wouldn't want these tissues, Miss Moody," she said quickly, patting her pocket. "These tissues are used. They are full of bogeys. Loads of bogeys. I have a cold," she went on. "A terrible cold. The worst cold ever. At-choo."

Rani shrank away from Isabel and her disgusting tissues. "I'm fine now, Miss Moody," she said. "I don't need a tissue. Especially not one of Isabel's."

The tissue trouble passed, but Isabel couldn't concentrate. Why exactly had she taken the

Our Beautiful Green Planet Intergalactic

Environmental Award trophy? It suddenly seemed like a very bad idea.

"The last word is *hideous*," said Miss Moody.

Isabel began to write hideous: h–i–d–e. . . But what came next?

She looked down at her test paper.

hide.

Hide.

Did the spelling test know what Isabel had done? Did it know what was hidden in her pocket right at this very moment?

No, decided Isabel. She was being silly. No one knew what she had done. Not even Lottie, who knew everything about everyone. Finally, Isabel had a secret that even the nosiest best friend in the world wasn't in on. It was quite a terrible secret, of course, and Isabel would have to make it right soon, or someone might find out. But Isabel was sure she could get away with it in the end.

Chapter

8

The Proof Is Not in the Pudding

Keeping a secret from Lottie proved to be hard work. Isabel's best friend loved a good mystery. The Case of the Vanishing Planet had Lottie's full attention. She spent most of the afternoon snooping around the front hallway, joined by Colonel Crunch, Mrs Peabody, Mrs Potion and Miss Biro. This meant that Isabel's plan to put the golden globe back became impossible.

By the end of the day, Lottie had gathered a number of clues. She found several apples that Colonel Crunch hadn't tidied up, a tiny shard of broken glass that hadn't been swept away

and a bit of fuzz on the floor near the pedestal. These were truly amazing real-life clues, but still there was no trace of the golden award itself. And most importantly, there was no reason for anyone to suspect Isabel.

"We searched everywhere, but it just isn't ANYWHERE!" Lottie told Zoe, Rani, Ava and Isabel. The friends had gathered round Lottie to try to help her solve the mystery. (Isabel, of course, was only pretending to help.)

"Because it's round, I knew the Our Beautiful Green Planet Intergalactic Environmental Award trophy might have rolled a long distance," said Lottie in her best detective voice. "But I've checked everywhere it could have fallen when Lady Lovelypaws jumped up."

"You mean down," said Isabel. She was trying to stand with her pocket as far away from Lottie as she could.

"Sorry?" asked Lottie.

"Lady Lovelypaws jumped down," said Isabel.

Lottie studied her closely. "How do you know that?"

So Lottie didn't know that Isabel had been at the scene of the crime. Colonel Crunch had just told Lottie that Lady Lovelypaws had crashed into the pedestal. He must not have said anything about Isabel being there in the hallway when the crash happened. There was no mention of Isabel in Lottie's notebook. This was a very good thing, if Isabel could only think of what to say next. Luckily, Ava spoke instead.

"It's the aliens," Ava said firmly. "I told you they were coming. They must've taken the award back with them into outer space."

Lottie considered this. She wrote it in her notebook. But it seemed unlikely. What would aliens want with the *Our Beautiful Green Planet Intergalactic Environmental Award*? Aliens weren't even *from* this planet.

"Maybe Lady Lovelypaws took the award?" suggested Rani.

Lottie liked this idea. It gave her a suspect. She wrote it down. The friends set off to find Lady Lovelypaws. It didn't take long: she was in Mrs Peabody's office, in the paper tray on the headmistress's desk. She had been so frightened by the crash that she had crawled *underneath* Mrs Peabody's papers.

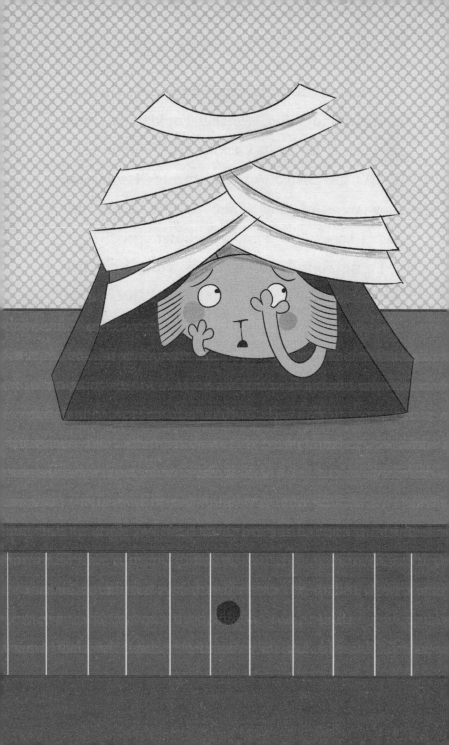

"She's been there all day," said Mrs Peabody sadly, stroking the papers. "She wouldn't even come out for a biscuit."

The *Our Beautiful Green Planet Intergalactic Environmental Award* trophy was not in the paper tray with Lady Lovelypaws.

"Lady Lovelypaws is innocent," declared Lottie. "But maybe someone else took the award. Someone human. Maybe it is not lost at all."

"It *is* real gold," added Rani.

Isabel did not like where this was going. This was starting to be a lot less fun than sneaking an ice lolly or making daisy chains.

The friends thought about the possibility that the award had been stolen. They studied Lottie's list of clues. (Well, four of them did. Isabel concentrated on her pocket. She felt hot. She needed to take her cardigan off but she didn't dare.)

"What if!!!" screeched Zoe, "What if, what if… Oh, I've got it!!! This is most definitely one hundred per cent what happened!!"

Isabel felt the wasps buzzing. Did Zoe know what she'd done? How could Zoe know?

"What is it???" gasped Lottie. "Out with it!"

"Whoever tidied up the apples must have tidied up the *Our Beautiful Green Planet Intergalactic Environmental Award* trophy by mistake!" shouted Zoe. "If we find the apples, we will find the gold!"

This was a brilliant idea. Lottie was extremely disappointed that she hadn't thought of it herself, and Isabel began to wish with all her heart that it were true. But, of course, Zoe's guess was wrong. When the girls got to the school kitchen they found that Mrs Crunch had already chopped up all the apples and put them in the crumble. Big trays of her famous pudding were cooling on the kitchen counter.

Four of the friends gasped. Had Mrs Crunch baked the *Our Beautiful Green Planet Intergalactic Environmental Award* trophy?

"Oh dear," said Isabel. "That's *terrible*. I suppose it is all melted and now it is gone forever. But at least we can stop looking, can't we?" Isabel had to get Lottie off the case.

Then Isabel noticed that Lottie was looking at her strangely. She put her hand over her pocket.

"But how will we know it was really in there?" demanded Lottie. "We'll have to investigate!" She grabbed a spoon and climbed up on the counter. She was just about to begin digging through the crumble for traces of real gold when a voice shouted, "FREEZE!"

Mrs Crunch was absolutely certain that she hadn't chopped up any *Our Beautiful Green Planet Intergalactic Environmental Award* trophies. She wasn't about to let her crumble be ruined for no reason. She ordered Lottie off the counter and shooed the girls out of the kitchen.

It was time to go home, and the mums were all waiting.

"Thank you for trying, girls," said Mrs Peabody sadly as they left. "It's just so odd. I don't know what on earth we are going to tell the mayor."

Isabel hadn't thought about the mayor.

Her pocket felt like the heaviest thing in the whole world.

Chapter

Where in the World Do You Hide the World?

Isabel had a new plan. It was too dangerous to put the *Our Beautiful Green Planet Intergalactic Environmental Award* trophy back, especially with Lottie on the case.

No, Isabel would just keep it. She'd keep the award forever and ever, until she was an old lady. No one would ever know. She would never get in trouble.

But where to hide it?

When she got home from school, Isabel set the Red alarm on her bedroom door and went straight to her secret hiding place: a glittery box that held all of her treasures. She kept it on a high shelf so the Reds couldn't get at it. Isabel took the golden globe from her pocket without looking at it, and tucked it into the box next to a jar of fairy dust from Ava's last birthday party. She shut the lid of the box and put it back on the shelf.

Isabel climbed down and sat on her bed. After a minute she climbed up again and took out the globe. She wrapped it in the tissue from her pocket, and she put it back. Just in case someone happened to discover her secret hiding place.

She sat on her bed again.

Isabel tried not to think about the award up there amongst all of her treasures.

She began to work on the igloo. She glued a few containers. The igloo walls were getting higher now. They were narrowing in to make the ceiling. She should have been enjoying this bit, now that the igloo was beginning to look like an actual igloo. But Isabel's eyes kept wandering back to the box on the shelf. Every time they did, Isabel remembered. She remembered what she had done.

This wouldn't do. She had got away with taking the golden globe, and now she needed to stop thinking about it. She had to get the *Our Beautiful Green Planet Intergalactic Environmental Award* trophy out of the special hiding-place box and far, far away, where she could forget about it. She climbed up on her bed, took out the golden globe and put it back in her cardigan pocket. Feeling the weight of it there again was truly terrible. How had this ever felt exciting?

Isabel put her wellies on and went out into the garden. Should she bury the *Our Beautiful Green Planet Intergalactic Environmental Award* trophy in the ground?

The trouble with that was that one of the Reds might dig it up. They loved digging holes in the garden, ever since Ava's little brother had buried loads of keys out there. They hadn't found all of the keys, so it was like an Easter egg hunt that never ended. Even Isabel's mum dug a hole every now and then, looking for her lost car key.

No, burying it in the garden would never do.

Isabel considered the rabbit hutch. No one but Isabel ever bothered with the pet bunnies any more. She could hide it in with Flopsy, Mopsy and Cottontail, and only think about it when she cleaned their cage.

But what if one of the bunnies ate it? Did rabbits eat real gold? And if they did, would real gold make them poorly? What if they got sick and it was Isabel's fault? What if they *died* and it was all because Isabel had stolen something? Then she would be a thief *and* a bunny killer.

Isabel went back into the house with the globe still in her pocket. She could hear the Reds watching *Peppa Pig*. Peppa and George were laughing and rolling in a muddy puddle, which meant that the episode was almost over. Isabel hurried back to her room. She put the bell on the door, pushed the rug under it and put *two* teddies on the chair. Then she went and sat in her igloo.

Isabel was miserable. She would never be rid of the *Our Beautiful Green Planet Intergalactic Environmental Award* trophy. She would have to carry it around in her pocket forever, and surely someone would catch her before too long. They would have to tell the mayor. The mayor was in charge of the police, so maybe Isabel would go to jail.

Suddenly the igloo felt very small. The milk-container walls seemed to be closing in on her. Was this what jail was like? Isabel looked up

...ards the top of the igloo, which was still unfinished. She wanted to see the ceiling of her cosy bedroom.

But instead she saw two brown eyes peering down at her.

"AHHHHHHHHHH!" Isabel screamed. "Lottie, how did you get in here?"

Isabel jumped up, her head poking out of the igloo's roof.

"Sorry," said Lottie. "I didn't mean to scare you."

"But ... but ... the alarm..." The Red alarm was set on the door. How had Lottie got into her room without Isabel hearing her?

Isabel didn't have the chance to ask, because Lottie was staring at something gold and shiny that was poking out of Isabel's pocket.

"Is that..." Lottie stared at the *Our Beautiful Green Planet Intergalactic Environmental Award* golden trophy.

What was there to say? That Isabel had just found it? That the aliens had dropped the golden globe from the sky and it happened to land in her pocket? Only Ava would have believed that. Isabel's heart was pounding in her chest and the wasps felt like they were in her throat.

"Yes," whispered Isabel. She could hardly speak.

"Where did you get it?" asked Lottie.

Isabel couldn't *lie* to her best friend. "I ... sort of ... took it," she said, her voice rising with every word. "I meant to put it back! But I can't get it back, because YOU are always in the hallway. And now I'm going to go to JAIL. You'll have to come play with me in JAIL!"

Lottie took her glasses out of her pocket. She put them on and looked at Isabel closely.

What would Lottie do? Surely she couldn't be Isabel's friend anymore. Stealing was such a terrible crime that Lottie would have to tell on Isabel. Maybe she really would call the police. Lottie would probably get an award of her own, for catching a real-life baddie.

Isabel held her breath.

"I know," said Lottie simply. "I knew it was you."

"What do you mean, *you knew it was me*?" cried Isabel. "How could you have known? Does everyone know?"

"No," said Lottie, "Just me. I solved the mystery and then I came round to find out why you did it."

It was impossible to know whether Lottie really had solved The Case Of The Vanishing Planet, or whether she'd just got lucky. All that was important to Isabel was that someone else knew her terrible secret, and that Lottie didn't seem to be about to tattle. Isabel told her the whole horrible story.

When she was finished, Lottie said, "I stole something once. I stole a sweetie from the Pick and Mix at the cinema."

"What kind of sweetie?"

"A pink sugar mouse."

That was a big sweetie to steal. "What happened?" asked Isabel.

"Mummy made me go up and pay for it," said Lottie. "And I said I was sorry and that I'd never do it again."

"Did you give it back?" asked Isabel.

"No," said Lottie. "Because it was in my tummy."

"Oh," said Isabel. It was a shame that she couldn't eat the *Our Beautiful Green Planet Intergalactic Environmental Award* trophy. That would get rid of it once and for all.

"Did you get into trouble?" she asked Lottie.

"Yes," said Lottie. "No sweeties for a week."

Isabel would have gladly traded no sweeties

for a week if she thought that would make up for what she'd done. She'd have had no sweeties for a year, even.

"This is different," she told Lottie. "This is real gold. The mayor's real gold. I might go to jail."

"Children don't go to jail," said Lottie. She sounded quite sure of herself.

"I might get expelled from school then," said Isabel. "Mrs Peabody might tell me to leave and never come back." No girl had ever been expelled from Crabtree School. Then again, no girl had ever stolen gold from the mayor before. It seemed a real possibility.

"We've got to put it back," said Lottie.

"But I don't know how to do that without getting caught!" said Isabel. She began to cry.

"I'll help you," said Lottie. "We can do it together."

"And you don't think I'm a terrible person?"

asked Isabel tearfully.

"No," said Lottie. "But I will have to keep a close eye on you to make sure you are good from now on."

Isabel looked at the Red alarm, which was still set on her bedroom door. How could Lottie keep a closer eye on her than she already did? But having your best friend watching over you is never a bad thing.

Chapter

Which Bin Do Golden Planets Go in?

The first thing Lottie did was to disguise the *Our Beautiful Green Planet Intergalactic Environmental Award* trophy. Before she left Isabel's house that evening, they covered the golden globe in papier mâché. That way Isabel could carry it round in her pocket and it would seem like a craft project she was working on. They hid the world under soggy newspapers, and it worked a treat, although now the planet was covered in goo.

Lottie was clever about disguises, but she wasn't quite as good at keeping secrets. Before the morning bell went the next day, Ava, Zoe and Rani all knew what Isabel had done. They gathered round the Year Three coat hooks.

"That's impossible," said Rani, when Lottie told her. "Isabel is the best-behaved girl at Crabtree School." Even Rani knew this, and she was the new girl.

Then Zoe joined their whispering. She remembered Isabel pushing in front of her in the queue. Ava remembered the daisy chains. Soon Isabel being naughty didn't seem so impossible.

When Isabel went to hang up her coat, her friends stared at her like they'd never seen her before. Straight away, Isabel could see that they all knew her secret, and she couldn't stand it.

"Stop staring! I already know that I'm the worst girl in the world!" cried Isabel. "No one has ever done anything as terrible as this in the whole history of Crabtree School!"

"Shhhhh!" Lottie told her. "You'll get caught!"

"People do bad things all the time," whispered Zoe. "Remember how mean I was to Rani when she came to Crabtree School?" They all nodded. In fact they had all done naughty things in the past; it was only Isabel who never had. Now she was just making up for lost time.

"Are you going to keep being naughty?" asked Zoe. "Because you can't come to my house to play if you are going to steal things."

"Mine either," agreed Rani. "Besides, if you steal from my brothers, they might hit you." Rani had four brothers, and the older ones were quite scary.

"Of course I am not going to keep being naughty!" said Isabel. "I am going to be even better than I was before."

They all nodded, though Isabel noticed that Ava looked disappointed. She had liked making daisy chains with the new naughty Isabel.

Once they were convinced that Isabel wasn't going to become a true baddie, the friends knew they had to help her. They spent morning break in the Crabtree School tree house making a plan to return the globe and keep Isabel from being expelled or thrown in jail. (Ava, for one, was sure that Lottie was wrong. Children *did* go to jail.)

"How about Rani, Ava and I distract them, and then Lottie and Isabel can put it back?" suggested Zoe.

"We could tell everyone that the aliens are finally landing. Then they will all rush to the windows to see!" added Ava.

Lottie frowned. "We can't just put it back on the pedestal now," she said. "We have to find a way of returning it without anyone knowing it was stolen. Otherwise they might still look for a suspect."

Everyone nodded in agreement.

"Let's just drop it in the playground when no one's looking," suggested Rani. "Then we can pretend to find it."

"I searched the playground yesterday and Colonel Crunch knows that," said Lottie. "It would be weird if it suddenly turned up, wouldn't it?"

They all nodded again, except for Zoe, who was standing on her head. Zoe thought better when she was upside down.

"What we need," said upside-down Zoe, "is to put it somewhere that it *might* have been yesterday, but that no one would have noticed. Somewhere we might have forgotten to look."

Lottie and Colonel Crunch and Mrs Peabody and Mrs Biro and Mrs Potion had searched the entire school from top to bottom, so there weren't many places they forgot to look.

Through the tree house window Isabel could see Colonel Crunch and Mrs Peabody chatting on the edge of the playground. Were they talking about the missing *Our Beautiful Green Planet Intergalactic Environmental Award* trophy? Were they guessing who might have taken it? Had they remembered that Isabel had been in the hall when Lady Lovelypaws jumped down? The wasps inside Isabel were buzzing and buzzing.

"I HATE this," cried Isabel, shaking her pocket. "I hate it, hate it, hate it!!! I wish I could just put this horrible, stupid *Our Beautiful Green Planet Intergalactic Environmental Award* trophy in the bin!"

"You know," said Lottie. "That just might work."

Zoe stood in front of the brightly coloured recycling bins. Blue, green, yellow and purple.

Blue was for plastic, she knew that. But Zoe wasn't quite as good at recycling as Isabel. Neither was Rani, who was standing next to Zoe at that moment. What were the other colours for again?

Zoe held the *Our Beautiful Green Planet Intergalactic Environmental Award* trophy gingerly between two fingers. She didn't want to touch it too much. She wanted to be rid of it NOW. But which bin was for real gold?

"Paper," decided Rani. "Put it in the bin for paper." That made sense, because even though they had peeled the papier mâché off the golden globe so that it would be findable, it still had bits of newspaper stuck to it. The paper bin would work just fine.

"That's the purple bin," said Zoe, and Rani didn't argue. They dropped the *Our Beautiful Green Planet Intergalactic Environmental Award* trophy into the purple bin and hurried

back to the Year Three classroom.

"The eagle has landed," Zoe said to Lottie. Zoe had no idea what eagles had to do with stolen awards. Lottie had told her that "the eagle has landed" is what spies say when they'd done what they were supposed to. Zoe had done it, so she said it.

"It's not in here," said Isabel without moving her lips.

"What do you mean, it's not in there? Of course it is. Zoe said 'the eagle has landed'." Lottie wasn't moving her lips either.

"IT REALLY ISN'T HERE!" Now Isabel was shouting without moving her lips, which is not an easy thing to do.

Their plan was not going to plan. At that very moment, Ava was leading Mrs Peabody to the little hallway off the kitchen. Then what was supposed to happen was this: Mrs Peabody would just happen to see Isabel finding the *Our Beautiful Green Planet Intergalactic Environmental Award* trophy in the recycling bin. The award would be returned. Mrs Peabody would be happy, and, instead of being expelled or sent to jail, Isabel would get praised for recycling.

It would have been a perfect plan, except the *Our Beautiful Green Planet Intergalactic Environmental Award* trophy wasn't actually *in* the recycling bin for Isabel to find.

"Try a different bin," hissed Lottie.

It is not very easy to dig through the rubbish in a busy hallway without being noticed. Lottie shook her head at Ava as she passed by with Mrs Peabody. They had to abandon the plan.

"Actually, Mrs Peabody," they heard Ava say to the headmistress, "never mind about coming to the kitchen. I just remembered that Mrs Crunch didn't *really* make the world's largest

104

jelly in the shape of Crabtree School. It was all a dream I had!" Ava and a very confused Mrs Peabody turned back towards the lunch room.

After a bit more digging, Isabel and Lottie gave up. They went back to their places at the Year Three lunch table.

"Which bin did you put it in?" Isabel asked Zoe and Rani frantically.

"Paper," whispered Zoe. "Like I told you. Purple for paper."

"Purple isn't for paper!!" said Isabel. "Purple is for food! You are meant to put the food you don't eat in there and Colonel Crunch takes it."

"Ewww!" said Rani. "Does he eat it?"

"Of course he doesn't eat it!" screeched Isabel. "He takes it out to the compost heap in the garden. The old food turns into soil for the plants."

"The purple bin didn't have food OR soil in it," said Lottie. "The purple bin was empty."

They all considered this. Then Lottie began flipping through the spy reports in her purple notebook.

"Colonel Crunch empties the purple bin all the time," said Lottie. "I've watched him do it. He takes the bin out to the compost heap and tips it in."

"That's what I just said!" hissed Isabel.

"What this means," said Lottie, ignoring her, "is that some time between Zoe and Rani putting the *Our Beautiful Green Planet Intergalactic Environmental Award* trophy in the purple bin, and lunchtime, Colonel Crunch emptied the purple bin."

"Which means," said Zoe, "that the eagle has landed out in the compost heap."

"Exactly," said Lottie. In a flash they were up from the table and headed for the field behind the playground.

Chapter

A Very Stinky Treasure Hunt

Isabel had never smelled anything so terrible in her entire life.

She was up to her knees in Mrs Crunch's fish pie. They'd had it for lunch yesterday, and now the uneaten bits from one hundred and fifty plates were rotting in the compost heap. There were carrot scrapings too, all slimy and slippery, and little mounds of squishy, squidgy peas.

Isabel would never eat fish pie again.

Lottie was digging through a mountain of spaghetti bolognaise. She had noodles stuck to

her skirt and a meatball on her head. There was stale garlic bread crunching under her feet.

"This compost heap," said Ava emerging from a sloppy puddle of last week's lasagne, "is probably what is keeping the aliens away. It smells DISGUSTING!"

"Oooo," said Zoe, pointing at a brown mound at the back of the compost heap. "Look, chocolate cake!"

"I think that's mud," said Rani. She was sifting through a pile of banana peels the size of a small house. Mrs Crunch liked to give them bananas as a snack.

There was no trace of the *Our Beautiful Green Planet Intergalactic Environmental Award* trophy. Isabel stopped digging and looked up at her friends. They were covered from head to toe in compost. And whilst compost is good for the environment and for making things grow, when it gets on your clothes it looks a lot like filthy muck. It smells even worse.

Isabel and her friends were going to get into a whole heap of trouble. And it would happen very soon, because Colonel Crunch had spied them in his compost pile. He was marching across the playground with Mrs Peabody close behind.

How would they explain why they were digging through the rubbish? Isabel's stomach was a hive full of wasps.

Then, out of the corner of her eye, Isabel saw a glint of shine through the muck. Could it be? Could it possibly be?

"I've FOUND IT!!!" screamed Isabel. "I've found the *Our Beautiful Green Planet Intergalactic Environmental Award!*" Isabel pulled the golden globe out of the compost and held it high above her head. As she waved it around, mashed potato dripped off the planet and into her hair.

"How on earth did it get out here?!" Mrs Peabody had reached the compost heap. She was beside herself with joy. "Oh, girls!! You are our heroes!!! Isabel Donaldson, I can't thank you enough! You are our newest Green Planet Golden Girl!"

Led by Colonel Crunch, the five stinky, filthy friends went on a victory march through the playground and back into the school. All around them, they heard the shouts and applause of

grateful Crabtree girls and their teachers.

"It's all over!" whispered Lottie to Isabel. "You won't be expelled, and you can forget you ever heard of the *Our Beautiful Green Planet Intergalactic Environmental Award!*"

But Isabel could not forget. Although the weight of the golden globe was no longer in her pocket, it felt like it was on her chest instead. The tummy wasps still wouldn't go away. Why wouldn't they go away now the award was back safely? She'd got away with stealing. Her friends had forgiven her, and she hadn't got into trouble. She was the best naughty girl in the whole world.

The problem was, Isabel didn't want to be naughty any more. From now on, she was going to be the old Isabel. She was going to be the best-behaved girl at Crabtree School.

There was another special assembly that

afternoon to tell everyone who hadn't already heard the good news: the *Our Beautiful Green Planet Intergalactic Environmental Award* trophy had been found by Isabel Donaldson, who had bravely searched the compost heap.

But when Mrs Peabody called out Isabel's name to thank her, Isabel didn't enjoy it one bit. What would Mrs Peabody say if she knew what Isabel had done? What if some day someone told her?

Isabel looked at Lottie, who was sitting beside her. Would Lottie remember to keep her secret? Had she written it down in her notebook? What if Lottie's mum read her notebook one day? Mums did things like that sometimes. Would Lottie's mum tell on Isabel?

How about Rani? Rani was sat on Isabel's opposite side. Isabel studied her closely. Rani was new – how well did Isabel know her *really*? Rani was loads of fun, but could she keep such a terrible secret forever? What if she couldn't?

Isabel could hardly stand to think about it.

Isabel was sure that she could feel someone looking at her. Who was watching her? Who knew? She scanned the room madly, until she saw two huge green eyes staring straight at her.

Lady Lovelypaws was staring at Isabel. Lady Lovelypaws knew exactly what she'd done. Isabel hadn't got away with it, not really.

"Lady Lovelypaws is a CAT," said Lottie. "She's not going to tell on you because she doesn't speak human."

"But she knows what I did," said Isabel sadly. "She was there. And all of you know, too."

Lottie, Isabel, Ava, Zoe and Rani were gathered round the coat hooks in the Year Three classroom again. They were getting their things together because it was nearly time to go home.

"We're not going to tell on you," said Ava. "We are your friends."

"But if you don't tell, then you are *lying!*" said Isabel, tears running down her cheeks. "I'm making my best friends tell lies!"

"It's not lying," said Rani, looking behind her to make sure no one was listening. "Nobody's asked us how we found the award, so it's not a lie, not really." She didn't sound too sure of herself.

"You're lying by not telling the truth," said Isabel finally. "And so am I."

Rani and Zoe began to discuss whether not telling something really counted as a lie, when it is really just keeping a secret. Lottie, however, was beginning to understand Isabel's problem. Some secrets were too big to keep in your notebook, or in your heart.

Isabel knew what she had to do.

Chapter

Biscuits, Mashed Potatoes
and Bubblegum

Mrs Peabody was delighted to have an afternoon visitor. It was the perfect time of day for a cup of tea and some biscuits. She made a big fuss over Isabel. She said over and over how grateful she was that the *Our Beautiful Green Planet Intergalactic Environmental Award* golden trophy had been found. Lady Lovelypaws glared at Isabel from Mrs Peabody's paper tray.

Isabel didn't want any biscuits. She squirmed in her chair. She didn't know how to say what she needed to say. She looked out of Mrs Peabody's window and saw Ava, Zoe and Rani peeking in from outside.

Knowing her friends were there made Isabel a bit braver.

"I did it," Isabel told Mrs Peabody. She spoke so quietly that Mrs Peabody could scarcely hear her.

"Sorry, dear?" the headmistress asked. "Did you say you did it? Did what, dear?"

"I DID IT." Isabel repeated. "I stole the *Our Beautiful Green Planet Intergalactic Environmental Award* golden globe trophy."

Mrs Peabody looked puzzled. She put down her cup of tea and her biscuit, and went into the hallway. Lady Lovelypaws stayed where she was on the desk, watching Isabel.

When Mrs Peabody came back she said, "I don't understand, darling. The award is right where it should be, safe and sound. All thanks to you," she said proudly. She picked up her tea.

"I found it," said Isabel. "But first, I took it. I put it in my pocket and I took it home. Then I brought it back and I threw it away."

Behind her teacup, Mrs Peabody's eyes went wide. She couldn't believe what she was hearing.

"Why would you do that?" asked Mrs Peabody. The kindest headmistress in all of Great Britain was not smiling any more.

Isabel tried to explain. She told Mrs Peabody all about Lucy Lu and recycling and not being chosen as the Our Green Planet Golden Girl. She told Mrs Peabody about colouring her hair with markers, about sneaking an ice lolly and about the daisy chains, though she left Ava out of that last bit. Then finally Isabel told Mrs Peabody how she'd picked up the *Our Beautiful Green Planet Intergalactic Environmental Award* trophy and decided not to put it back.

"But that is *stealing*, Isabel," said Mrs Peabody.

"I know," said Isabel. Tears were welling in

her eyes, but she dared not let them out. Mrs Peabody could not bear to see a child cry. Isabel wondered if Mrs Peabody could hear the wasps in her tummy, and whether those would upset the headmistress too.

Ava, Zoe and Rani had their faces smashed right up against the windowpane. They were desperate to know what would happen to their friend.

"Am I going to be expelled?" asked Isabel fearfully. She had never seen Mrs Peabody look as stern as she did at that moment.

"No," said Mrs Peabody finally.

They heard a cheer from outside the window, and one from above their heads too. Isabel and Mrs Peabody gasped as Lottie dropped down from the chandelier that hung over the headmistress's desk. She landed on the rug in front of them.

"Good gracious, Lottie!" shrieked Mrs

Peabody. "You nearly gave me a heart attack."

"Thank you SO MUCH for not excluding my best friend," said Lottie to Mrs Peabody. "Thank you, thank you, thank you—"

"That's quite enough, Lottie," said the new stern Mrs Peabody. "Isabel and I need to finish our conversation. Please go and join your friends outside my window."

Lottie went.

"Are you going to tell the mayor what I've done?" asked Isabel. "He might send me to jail."

"The mayor is a *she*," said Mrs Peabody. "And *she* has lots of important things to do, so we won't bother her with this issue."

"What's going to happen to me?" asked Isabel.

"Oh, Isabel," sighed Mrs Peabody. "It's terribly naughty to steal, but I think you know that now. And it was very, *very* brave of you to tell me the truth."

"Mrs Peabody, can you ever forgive me?" Isabel couldn't bear this serious new headmistress.

Mrs Peabody looked at Isabel. Then she looked at Lady Lovelypaws. The cat and the headmistress seemed to be thinking things over. Then after ages and ages, they both nodded a bit and turned to face Isabel.

"Isabel Donaldson," said Mrs Peabody. "I am very disappointed in you for taking the *Our Beautiful Green Planet Intergalactic Environmental Award* globe from its place. I would never have imagined that you would do something like that." Lady Lovelypaws shook her head from side to side.

"But you are very sorry, aren't you, Isabel?" asked Mrs Peabody.

"Yes," cried Isabel. "I'm so sorry! I feel terrible! I have these angry wasps buzzing in my tummy all the time."

"Then the important thing, *the most important*

thing in all of this," said Mrs Peabody, "is to remember that feeling. Remember those wasps. They will tell you when you've done something wrong, and they won't go away until you've made it right."

"The wasps are horrible," said Isabel. "I wish they would go away forever."

"No," said Mrs Peabody firmly. "You don't wish that. You need them. Sometimes people ignore those wasps in their tummies, a little bit here and a little bit there, and then the wasps fly away forever. Then you are left not knowing right from wrong. That's when the trouble really starts."

"I won't ignore the wasps again," said Isabel. "I promise. I just wish I could take it all back!" Tears dripped on to Isabel's cheeks. Mrs Peabody, who was beginning to panic at the sight of Isabel crying, gave a nod to Lady Lovelypaws. The cat leapt from the paper tray and rubbed against Isabel's feet.

Mrs Peabody smiled kindly, like her old self. "If this is the worst thing you ever do in your life, Isabel Donaldson, then you will be quite all right. I forgive you. But for your punishment, you will help Colonel Crunch with the composting for the rest of the term."

"Yes, of course," said Isabel.

"Then you will give the Reception class a presentation on how composting works," said Mrs Peabody. "Perhaps Lucy Lu might want to help you." Isabel nodded.

"Now," continued Mrs Peabody, "let's get you off home, where you can have a bath. You smell like rotten mashed potatoes." The headmistress sniffed the air again. "And bubblegum."

"I must say, Isabel," Mrs Peabody added. "I do rather like this wild pink hair of yours. But not for school, you understand?"

Isabel understood.

Isabel asked Lottie, Ava, Zoe and Rani to come to her house after school. None of them smelled very nice, but not being expelled seemed worth celebrating.

After a good hand-washing and a quick snack, the girls went upstairs to Isabel's room. That's when she noticed it: the tape had been peeled off the outside of Isabel's bedroom door. It was crumpled in a little ball on the floor. Scarlett and Ruby were cowering in the hallway looking very guilty.

Normally, Isabel would have screamed for their mum. But now she understood what it felt like to do something terrible and to wish you could take it back. Isabel told the Reds never to do it again. She could tell from the looks on their faces that they wouldn't.

Then, Isabel did something very kind. She invited the Reds in to work on the igloo with the big girls. Whilst they glued, Isabel and her friends each took turns colouring a little piece of their hair with the scented markers. Zoe went for purple, Rani chose yellow to show up in her dark hair, and Ava did green because the aliens would like it. Isabel added a red stripe to her pink hair.

This time, the girls only coloured a small section of the underneath bit of their hair, so it wouldn't be quite as naughty. Before they started colouring, Isabel checked in with her tummy. The wasps were quiet; they liked a bit of mischief as much as anyone.

Later that evening as the sun went down, Isabel, Zoe, Lottie, Ava and Rani sat inside the finished igloo. With Isabel watching closely, the Reds had coloured the milk containers every shade in the rainbow. Now the light inside the igloo was green and pink and orange and yellow and red.

Isabel thought it was the most beautiful place on the planet, and her friends agreed.

Turn the page
for lots more
Crabtree School
fun!

ALL ABOUT ME

MY FULL NAME: Isabel Elizabeth Donaldson

WHERE I LIVE: I live at Number 62, Cherry Tree Lane

WHAT MY ROOM LOOKS LIKE: My room is tidy and there is A LOT of craft stuff. It is white and red and pink mostly. There is also some blue and a bit of green. And purple.

WHO IS IN MY FAMILY: My family is me, Mummy, Daddy and the Reds (real names Scarlett and Ruby).

MY PETS: We have three bunnies called Flopsy, Mopsy and Cottontail. We had Peter but he ran away because Ruby left the bunny hutch open. ☹

MY BEST FRIEND(S): My best friends are Lottie, Ava, Zoe and Rani.

WHAT I LOVE TO DO: I love to make things especially things you can play with, like conker people. I am very good at drawing and painting and sewing and sticking. I am also good at ballet.

WHAT MAKES ME CROSS:
MY SISTERS GOING IN MY ROOM!!!!

WHAT I AM MOST AFRAID OF: Doing something really naughty.

WHAT I COLLECT: Ribbons, sweetie wrappers, pencil shavings, toilet-paper tubes, empty bottles, safety pins, old birthday candles, conkers, milk containers, corks, confetti, ice-lolly sticks, photos from magazines, leaves, dried flowers, stones

MY SECRET HIDING PLACE: A special box high on a shelf. The box has lots of glitter.

ISABEL'S REWARD CHART
FOR A HAPPY LIFE

Sometimes star charts are for practising piano and tidying up, but this one is a little bit different! Colour in a star for each good deed you do!

	Mon	Tues	Wed	Thurs	Fri	Sat	Sun
Make up a silly dance	☆	☆	☆	☆	☆	☆	☆
Play with someone new during break time	☆	☆	☆	☆	☆	☆	☆
Give a friend a hug	☆	☆	☆	☆	☆	☆	☆
Tell a funny joke	☆	☆	☆	☆	☆	☆	☆
Give yourself a big smile in the mirror	☆	☆	☆	☆	☆	☆	☆
At bedtime, think of something you did really well today	☆	☆	☆	☆	☆	☆	☆

ISABEL'S TOP TIPS FOR SAVING THE PLANET

1) Recycle. Know which bin everything goes in!

2) If you can, walk, cycle or scoot to school instead of going in a car

3) Make beautiful art out of old cereal boxes, ice-lolly sticks, kitchen-roll tubes, newspapers, yoghurt pots...

4) Grow a beautiful flower, outside in the garden if you have one, or inside the house

5) Turn off the lights when you leave a room! (Unless someone's still in there, of course!)

Can you think of another Top Tip for Saving the Planet? Write it here:

_____

_____

ISABEL IS BUILDING AN IGLOO TO PLAY IN. WHAT KIND OF MAGICAL HIDEOUT SHOULD YOU MAKE? TAKE THE QUIZ TO FIND OUT, AND THEN LET YOUR IMAGINATION RUN WILD!

1. Which activity sounds like the most fun?
a. Swimming
b. Visiting an adventure playground
c. Going to the beach
d. Hot-air balloon ride

2. Which present would you like to receive?
a. Roller skates
b. Spy set
c. Craft kit
d. Story book

3. Which magical creature would you like to meet?
a. Mermaid
b. Elf

c. Unicorn

d. Fairy

4. What magical ability would you like to have?

a. Invisibility

b. Speaking to animals

c. X-ray vision

d. Flying

5. What's your favourite ice cream topping?

a. Hundreds and thousands

b. Chocolate flake

c. Caramel sauce

d. Mini marshmallows

6. What's your favourite time of year?

a. Winter

b. Autumn

c. Summer

d. Spring

7. Where's the best hiding place for your secret things?

a. A hole in the tree at the bottom of your garden

b. Inside the trophy you won at school

c. You're not telling!

d. A special silver box at the back of your drawer

8. What would your friends say about you?

a. You're always kind

b. You're really helpful

c. You're very brave

d. You have a big imagination

THE RESULTS

Mostly As: Make an underwater palace in your cupboard!

You'll love pretending to live in a beautiful palace in the deep blue sea! You will be surrounded by all the friendly creatures of the ocean – dolphins, pretty fish and mermaids. Your palace will be made of the prettiest coral ever seen, and your bed will be a giant, cosy shell that fits you perfectly.

Mostly Bs: Make a castle with a cardboard box!

You can dream up a fantastic castle, and with your imagination add secret tunnels, majestic towers with views across the land, and more rooms than you'll ever have time to explore! You'll be able to throw parties for everyone in the kingdom, but make sure you keep a lookout for invading little brothers and sisters.

Mostly Cs: Make a tropical island with a blanket in the garden (or in the sitting room!)

You can create a tropical island surrounded by palm trees, coconuts, hammocks and the lovely sea, where you'll spend your afternoon playing games and dancing around pretend campfires on the beach. If you get too hot, go for a pretend swim.

Mostly Ds: Make a city in the clouds with some pillows!

Why stay on earth when you could live in the clouds? You can float away and watch the earth from your fluffy cloud pillow, which is the most comfortable place you can possibly imagine. You'll make friends with the birds and leap from cloud to cloud to visit all your friends.

CRABTREE SCHOOL

Collect all the Crabtree School books!

Win a family set of scooters!

To celebrate the brilliant Crabtree School series we've got four brand new Micro Scooters® to give away! The lucky winner will also receive a signed set of four Crabtree School books.

Scooting as a family is the perfect way to spend quality time together; you can travel in style and then snuggle down at story time with the Crabtree School gang. Ideal for lots of family fun, you won't want to miss out on this amazing prize!

Visit **www.crabtreeschool.com** to enter the free competition before it closes at midnight on 31st December 2015.

Good luck!

*T&Cs apply – visit **www.crabtreeschool.com** for full details